SIDNAAZ (FANFICTION)

FANFICTION OF TRENDING COUPLE SIDHARTH SHUKLA AND SHEHENAZ GILL.

ASMA TAHIR

Copyright © Asma Tahir
All Rights Reserved.

This book has been published with all efforts taken to make the material error-free after the consent of the author. However, the author and the publisher do not assume and hereby disclaim any liability to any party for any loss, damage, or disruption caused by errors or omissions, whether such errors or omissions result from negligence, accident, or any other cause.

While every effort has been made to avoid any mistake or omission, this publication is being sold on the condition and understanding that neither the author nor the publishers or printers would be liable in any manner to any person by reason of any mistake or omission in this publication or for any action taken or omitted to be taken or advice rendered or accepted on the basis of this work. For any defect in printing or binding the publishers will be liable only to replace the defective copy by another copy of this work then available.

This book is dedicated to Sidharth Shukla, His humbleness made me to write a fanfiction on him. When the whole world was sad with his sudden demise, I thought to write.

Tomy lovely family and my world's best teachers,

for always loving and supporting me.

I couldn't repay, what they have done to me

even with a lifetime of dog treats.

but I'll try anyway.

yours writer,

Asma Tahir

Contents

Preface

Preface

Hello I'm Asma,

This book is a fanfiction of legend Sidharth Shukla & Shehnaz Gill.

Their bonding in Bigboss is just awesome but unfortunately Sidharth was died, for this sudden dismise of him made fans disappoint. So, this made me to write this beautiful fanfiction on them.

Thank you so much for choosing my book. I know there are lot of stories, and it means great deal to me that you picked up one of mine, and choose to spend time with characters I created. Ever since I was a little kid, I knew I wanted to be a writer, and having readers like you is a dream come true.

CHAPTER ONE

Sidnaaz ? Shehnaz look at here, I have a surprise for you....

What's that dad ? What... Application of Delhi University. Oh really ? Unbelievable dad...I love you ? But... Where should I stay ? I mean we are living in Bombay.

No problem dear, your dad's friend house is there. You can stay there... What ?I can't stay in Shaikar uncle's house, how can I ? Don't worry dear, they will take care of you...

Bell rang? Yesss coming.... Who's that? Oh... namaste? uncle aunty ji. Who's that shehenaz ? Oh... Mr Shekhar & Mrs Shekhar welcome welcome....

We were just talking about you. Oh really ! What's that ? Actually, Shehenaz wanna join Delhi University. So we were just thinking were she will...

It's just simple dear, she will stay in our home. (Mrs Shaikar)

No no... We don't wanna bother you.

There is nothing will bother us...

Have some coffee, please(Shehnaz)

Thanks dear So, what's the plan dear... I mean career. Oh... That's nothing big uncle, just wanna be a software engineer. Oh really,That's good.

Thanks aunty...

Even Abhishek is in the same field.

Oh ... Sorry to ask, who's he ?

You don't remember him? You and he used to play in childhood, Even he used to ask about you, like you're still the same stubborn Shehnaz and chubby, who use to cry often without any reasons. Shehnaz still the same sensitive girl, like she used to be in her childhood.

Shehnaz pov

How can someone remember, someone's childhood behaviour.It's just stunning. He remembers everything about me, and here I am don't even remember him.how bad memory you have Shehnaz...

She was busy with her chain of thoughts and was interrupted by her uncle.

So finally I decided that Shenaz is coming with us.(Mr Shaikar)

No uncle, I will come later... I agree with my friend's dicision.

No more excuses dear,

but uncle....

No means no excuses dear. Now pack and come, good girl.

Bye mom & dad, take care Good bye?

After few hours

Shehnaz dear, we are reached. Wow... Unbelievable ???

The beautiful house which make her stun....

Welcome shehenaz mam....(servent)

Can you please show her room, she must be tired.(Mrs Shaikar)

Sure Mrs Shekhar (servent) Yeah you're right.

so let her take rest, we will introduce to everyone about her later....

No no... Uncle I am not that much...

I think you're eyes is not supporting to your mouth, they were clearly telling how much tired you're. Mam please come with me.

I will show you, your room.

after coming room

Yeah.... Oh God... I am so tired, everything is blur to me except the bed... First I wanna shower next I have to rest.

•3•

CHAPTER TWO

After few hours

Yes... Come in

Mam... Mrs Shekhar is calling you.

Yeah, I will... You can go.

How you're feeling now ?

Feeling better aunty ji.

So, let me introduce you to everyone.

This is your uncle, I think you know him verry well.? Namaste ? Me uncle's wife, this is mamy (aunty)of Abhishek and this is her daughter Suman. Namaste ? And...

That's all?(Shehnaz)

No no... There is a main person to be introduced.

Who ?

Abhishek...

Oh... Where is he ?

He is in Australia, I will introduce him in video call.

It's okay aunty ji... No problem.

And... This is Naina (secretary) and she will be with you anytime you want help, you can ask her...

Yes mam, please don't hesitate to ask any help.

Thanks ☺? Thank you sooo much aunty ji?

You're always welcome ☺?

Shehnaz pov

Oh no... I forgot to call my mom, she told me to call after I reached. She must be waiting... Ringing mom....... Hello mom

Idiot, don't I told you to call ?

Sorry mom... Uncle and aunt ji is so kind, I am verry thankful to them.

Oh... So you forget us

No mom, you're not getting my point.

By the way, I told you that they will take care.

Yes mom, you're right. ☺?

After few minutes

Ok byeeee mom I am feeling sleepy...

Good night my dear...

First meet accidentally with Sid...?

In the morning She just check herself in mirror and went to dinning hall for breakfast.

Namaste ? uncle aunty ji

God bless you dear?

And she went near Suman chair and say namaste ? as loud as audible to her, but she didn't response and give her a disgusting look. Shehnaz was shocked by her weird behaviour towards her and later ignore it. To break the awkward silence, she told "today is my first day in college and I don't want to be late, so I am leaving...

Have a great day ahead dear ☺?

Thank you so much ?

Wait... I will tell my driver to drop you.

No thanks uncle, I will go by walk. And as well I wanna lose my weight.

Yeah... You should, otherwise you would look like elephant (Suman murmured to herself) Except Shehnaz, no one hear... She just ignored and leave...

CHAPTER THREE

Shehnaz pov

What the hell, why she's behaving like this, I don't know what's the problem she have with me...

Uff.... Are you blind, can't you see. 5.5 feet I am I. You were just about to hit me, what will happen if you...(Shehnaz)

Enough is enough ? It was good luck to you, I didn't hit. Don't you have any manners to walk ?(Sidharth)

Oh... You're going to teach me, who even don't know how to drive car in streets.

You... How dare you ? You mean I wanna proof ? How much dare I have ?(Sidharth)

Oh... Girl just stop this...

I have urgency, so let me go.

She said same here and leave. She went to college, thankfully she wasn't late. She meet some of her Bombay friends and enjoy her first day in college with full of joy.

Shehnaz pov

How much rude he was, inner voice but he was handsome too (more than required) Stop it shehenaz stop it... You should control yourself ?

After few hours

How was your day dear ?

It was just awesome aunty ji?

I think you're must be tired, so I will bring something to you to eat.

Yeah sure... As am starving to eat as the smell hit my nose?

Ha ha ha Just two minutes I will bring... Aunty ji Food was delicious ? Thank you so much... Your welcome dear... Ok go and take rest.

Ok bye. Wait dear... I want to tell you something, What's that?

Actually we are going to marriage, so if you're interested you can come with us.

No... Aunty ji, I have to prepare for test. So, I can't. I will stay with Naina... Ok as your wish dear?

CHAPTER FOUR

Next morning

Shehnaz pov

Ufff... I forget that I am alone with Naina. I think, I should go to kitchen to make coffee.

Good morning mam (Naina)

Good...

Mam what you like to eat in breakfast? so I will be able to inform them.

Nothing special... Tell me what you like the most to eat in breakfast?

Ma'am.......

Tell?

She said with hesitance Sandwich

Good simple, tell Sandwich to them.

Yummy ? It's not it?

Yes ma'am...

Ufff... Don't call me ma'am, you can call me Shehnaz.

Ok ma'am, sorry Shenaz.

Hmmm So good....

Shehnaz pov

Why this room is locked, I think it's not mine... Oh...it's going to open.

Oh... You idiot....(Shehnaz)

You cheaper...(Sidharth)

Mind your words Mr arrogant.

No one ever told you that whenever we enter to someone's room we should knock. You can't come without their permission.(Sidharth)

Oh... Don't anyone teach to ask permission before entering someone's house and now you came to room also. Just disgusting ?

Hey.... What do you think about you?

Oh... Don't you know? Mr Shekhar uncle's friend daughter.

I am Shehnaz. And you? I am Sidharth, son of Mr Shekhar. ??? I am Sidharth Shukla, son of Mr Shekhar. ???

Ha ha ha You must be joking, l am l right? By the way, I really wanna appreciate your sense of humour.

Shehnaz... Shehnaz (Naina call her from kitchen)

I am coming... Wait a minute, I will be back Mr arrogant.

What Naina ?

Coffee ?

Oh... You really made for me ?

Ofcourse (Naina)

Can you give me one more cup of coffee please ?

She look lil bit surprised.but manege herself and said surely.

Shehnaz take two cup of coffee and went to Sidharth room.

Oh... You brought coffee for me?

Anyway thanks ?

Oyee... I didn't made coffee, it was made by Naina.

When I told you made ?

I just wanna clarify, nothing more than that...

Hmmm

Shehnaz dear.... (Mrs Shekhar call her)

Oh... I think they were back, I am leaving. And one more thing, you thief don't dare to theft anything and just leave.

Because Mrs Shekhar came home. ???

What ? What you said? I am thief and I will dare to theft your belongings ? Are you mad ? have you lost it?

Anyway bye... Mrs Shekhar is calling and I have to leave. Miss stubborn....

What? Don't you dare to call me like that.

Could you do a favour for me Please ?

What favour ???

After leaving, please lock the door from outside and don't tell anyone about me and my visit please.

Ok...but if I lock from outside then how can you... Oh.... You really worrying about me, Awwww

Stupid ?.... Nothing like that. Uffff... I am getting late bye.

She went out of the room and locked it successfully. Suddenly she saw Mrs Shekhar coming in her way, she feels lil nervous.

Oh... You are finally here dear, I was searching for you from last ten minutes. By the way why are you here?

Aahh..... Mrs Shekhar sensed her nervousness and she don't wanna bother her. So she said, ok leave it dear... I came here to introduce you with someone ☺?

Shehnaz pov

Who's he? I mean Mr arrogant Is really son of Mr Shekhar ? He can't be... Because Shekhar uncle and aunty ji were soft character. He is totally different from them, how can it be possible? If he said true means ? Then why aunty ji didn't tell about him or introduce him. What if she's going to introduce about him tomorrow. Yeah... Because she told, I am going to introduce you with someone. What if the someone is Mr Sidharth no no... Mr arrogant ? Ok.... Why I give coffee to him? What will he think about me? Did he really mean when he calls me cheaper ???? Uff... Why even I am I thinking about him ? I should stop thinking and I have to sleep.

Sidharth pov

How beautiful she's and lil bit innocent no no.... Stubborn girl. And what she told me? Thief ? Oh my god, save me from her stubbornn

pov ends

What's up bro? Why are you simileing ? Oh... Bhabhi.....

Stop it Asim... I wanna ask you something.

Ask. I am all here.

I am I looking like a thief to you?

What? Who said this to world handsome bachelor ?

Asim.... I am serious here

No no... Why?

Nothing special, just ask.

Oh... You're not going to tell me, ok.

you never treat as a bestfriend, i know i am not you're bestfriend.

stop this emotional blackmail...

i'll tell.

CHAPTER SIX

Ok.... Naina, can you please sleep with me. Even we became good friends, so if you stay with me for a night then we will get to know each other verry well.(Shehnaz)

Oh really.... Ok

Thank you so much ?

Can you please tell me, who's he?

Who Shehnaz ?

I mean Mr Sidharth Shukla.

Naina give pale expression to her, as someone snatch something secret from her. Who knows? (Naina)

You know idiot tell me...

I will tell you but you first promise me that you will help him.

Help.... whom?

Hmm.... Sidharth Shukla. You expect me to help him, I mean to Mr arrogant ? Never ever...

Then fine... I am not to tell you, Goodnight...

Ok ok... I will try. Now tell me please. Who's he? And why he's visit shouldn't be known to anyone? What's the relationship he sharing with Mr Shekhar uncle ?

Now listen carefully Shehenaz ? (Dark secret...................) ?????

How dare her to harm Mr Sidharth. Suman must had think that no one will fight for him. But I am here to fight for him....

Next day

Good morning uncle aunty ji...

Good...

Dear Shehnaz wait... Where are you going Without breakfast ?

Sorry uncle...I will eat in canteen, I am already late.

On the way to home

Oyeee... Mr arrogant

Ufff... This girl never leave me in peace ? Don't I mentioned my name?

Yeah... But this name suits you better ?

Why you called me?

Actually, I wanna tell you something.

Tell me I am all here

I can't say here, can we go to cafe... I want to tell you something important.

But... I am not interested...

What...? What you mean you're not interested ?

I meant to it what I say...

Please ? listen to me, it's important...

Ok... I will meet you tomorrow in this same time.

Are you sure ?

Dam sure...

Ok.... Then bye.

Good bye ◆

CHAPTER SEVEN

Next day

Miss stubborn....

Hmm... Come with me Shehnaz...

Yeah, I am coming....

In the cafe

Hmm...tell now.

Actually, I know about your secret ?

He look at her shock?

Yeah... You heard right...

What you know about me ? That I am murderer of my grandmother.

No no... I know the truth one.

What?

Your enemy Suman, murder your grandmother by adding poison in her drink and handover it to you. And blamed you that... You murder your grandmother because she told that she will give her more than half property to your elder brother. So you get joleous and take this step. Like that she tell everyone that you're the murderer...

So, I wanna help you.

What will you do ? You will tell them . That... I did nothing?

No no... I will proof them ☺?

I don't want your help ? If I would have known that you are going to tell this means I never would have visit with you.

What you mean, you won't ??? I am telling you to help and here you showing your attitude ? (Shehnaz)

Keep your pity help with you, I don't want. Show to them, who actually need this.(Sidharth)

What is this behaviour Mr arrogant ?

Don't you dare...

I will call you, do whatever you want.

Ahhh... Leave my wrist Sidharth... It's hurting....

Let it hurt, I hurt more than this.... And Now leave this cafe... Stop your drama.

Sidharth you hurt me and I am never gonna forget this....

Thank you.... Shehnaz.

How can someone be this much hurtles? Whoever send him out of the house, they take verry good dicission. What I told him that he get hurt ? Nothing I use harsh words to hurt him then why ? He is such a arrogant ? I never ever gonna talk to him even if he please. Did he even bother to ask sorry ?

Sidharth what happen ?(Asim)

You're looking so sad today. Is everything is ok????

No... Asim?

What you mean??? I hurt her verry badly,

Whom? Why?

Shehnaz. She's still stranger to me and she suddenly started talking about my dark past and even told that she will help me.... So my ego got hurt.

What ? If someone wants to help you means why your ego is hurting? I am not getting you Sidharth.

Because I don't want to look pity and weak in her eyes.

So... Hmmm... Do one thing... Ask her sorry, simple.

No no.... I can't...

There is no other idea than this. Just ask sorry... It's not a big deal, don't you know that "If you're wrong admit it" "If you're right then shut your mouth ?"

Asim.... I am serious here.

Okay... Tomorrow I will try. Hmm... Good boy. Now let me sleep please Sidharth.

Okay.. Good night. ?

Uff... This Asim ☺

CHAPTER EIGHT

Himanshi....(Shehnaz)

What Shehnaz ?

He hurt me...

Who? And why???

Mr arrogant ? Because I ask him to help. I think he must mad....

Ha ha ...(Naina) Shehnaz.... Not like that, he must be in bad mood. So he hurt you and trust me, he must never intended to hurt you.

How can you say so confidently ????(Himanshi)

Because I know him verry well ☺?

I see...(Shehnaz)

Asim... Wake up.

What ???

Sid... Idiot tell me how should I ask sorry?

Hmm... Open your mouth and move your tonque like this and just lil bit loud. And say sorry, just simple?

Idiot..... I am gonna kill you ?

Then what Sid ? Just say it that's all ?

Ok... I am leaving. Bye...

CHAPTER NINE

Shehnaz... Please ? listen... Shehnaaaaaz...(Sidharth)

Don't you dare to talk to me.

Please I am really sorry, Please come with me, we will talk..

Nothing left to talk... Now leave me...

Please listen once, I am really so so sorry ?

Finish???? Now let me go.

Shehnaz.... What ? Come with me...

No... No..

I will see how will you disobey me...(Sidharth)

No... You can't force me to come with you.(Shehnaz) I will make noise and I will let people handle you.(Shehnaz)

You're blackmailing me ?(Sidharth)

No... Warning you.(Shehnaz)

Ok... Do want you can.(Sidharth)

Oh... Help me, help me.(Shehnaz)

Hey what's happening? (People)

Nothing... She's my wife, she's angry with me so she's making drama.????

Aahh... ?? Now please wifey Could you please come with me ? ???

yes . . .

CHAPTER TEN

Sidnaaz date???

What should I wear for dinner? No...no. date? Yeah... This suits me. Naina... How I am l looking ?

Looking like a angel.

Oh really ?

Sss Ok... Bye I am getting late.

After few minutes

Hi... Hello.. How are you Shehnaz?

As good as can be?

What about you?

Hmm... Good.

Today you're looking gorgeous ? When God made you, he was really showing off? Sidharth

Thanks ?

And ... How I am I looking?

Hmm... Good Just good??

Hmm... Sidharth....

Sss.. tell I here. Actually, why Suman added poison in juice? I mean, why she did?

Shehnaaaz... Can we talk about this later?(Sidharth)

I wanna know more about you. So tell me something about you.(Sidharth)

Hmm... About me ?

Ss ....about you

Well... Name Shehnaz Age 24, Height 5.5, Fav person mom & dad Trust mom & dad Fear of darkness and betrayed ? Hmm...and Education MCA Career software engineer, Fav food fast food (pani puri) Fav colour every colour (based on things) Zodiac Aquarius Uff.. girl your given your whole bio data? ? Shehnaz Ok.... Tell something about you

Hmm... Name Sidharth Shukla Age 28 Education MBA Career Business Fear of .... Your stubbornness ? .... Nothing Trust no one Fav person my best friend Asim Oh.... Nice Fav food and colour? I think no use of telling you.

Why? Because you're not my.... Gf ?

After few minutes of awkwardness Ok... How's your business going?

Not bad... Hmm.... They talk simply.... After few minutes

Sidharth said I think we should leave now. It's already late... Your Aunty ji must waiting for you... Hmm... Your right.

Wait... I will drop you.

No...no . What if someone see you?

No one will.

Ok... Stop stop...

Why? Uncle is coming, so it's better if you drop me here.

Ok... As your wish. Bye....

Good bye.. Take care Shehnaz.?

Author's note Sid - Sidharth

Naaz - Shehnaz

CHAPTER ELEVEN

Naaz - mom dad.... What a surprise ? You're here.

Dad - where are you coming from late night?

Naaz - actually, I went to my friend house.

Mom - but... When you're in Bombay you never go to meet your friend in house. So now what happen?

Mammy (aunt) - nowadays childrens are so irresponsible, we should keep an eye on them. Because we don't know, what they are doing in our back ?

Naaz - mammy (aunt) what are you trying to say? Say it clearly.

Mom - Shehnaz... Don't you know how to talk with elders???

Mammy (aunt) - leave it sister... She don't know.... Look at my daughter she's Shehnaz age but she never ever come home late night, it's all about upbringings.

Naaz - mind your words aunt....

Mom - shehenaz.....? Go to your room.

After few minutes

God... What the hell is happening ? Please help me.... God

Next morning

Sid - wait Shehnaz...... I will drop you.

Naaz - no need... Sid - why what happen?

Naaz - stay away from me.

Sid - what ???

Naaz - people started to talk about us so, it's better we should stop meeting eachother. Bye...

In evening at home Phone ringing.... Naaz

CHAPTER TWELVE

Naaz - new number hmm... Who's this ?

Naaz - hello Person - hi... Naaz - who's this ?

Person - your nightmare

Naaz - uff... You Sidharth.

Sid - haha Sss

Naaz - why you call?

Sid - actually, I think there's no problem in talking in phone.

Sid - the people can't find it like we are.... Friends. So... You can speak... And no need to worry.

Naaz - so...

Sid - so... We can speak.

Naaz - you call me to tell this ?

Sid - no... Just I wanna talk to you.

Naaz - tell ... Sid - from tomorrow I will drop you college.

Naaz - what ? Why ? Sid - what you mean why? Is there's any problem?

Naaz - Sss what if anyone see... Sid - no one will ?

Naaz - how? Sid - because I will drop you in car.

Naaz - I am not coming...

Sid - no.... You will

Naaz - I see...

Sid - bye...

Naaz - good bye...

Next day

On the way to college Shehnaz... Come I will drop you Hmm...

Sid - you have always problem that what people think if you're with me. But.... If you with him... there's no problem... I am right.

Naaz - with whom...? I didn't get your point.

Sid - you know verry well, whom I am talking about.

Naaz - seriously I don't know...

Sid - I am talking about..... Abhinandan.

Naaz - oh... He's my friend.

Sid - stay away from him...

Naaz - Are you trying to order me ?

Sid - may be...

Naaz - what you think, I will obey you ?

Sid - you should ....

Naaz - what I am I to you? What you think ???

Sid - ?

Naaz - don't dare to order me, I am leaving....

In college

Naaz - Himanshi.... My friend...

Himan - how are you?

Naaz- hmmm .... Fine. I am thinking?how Sidharth get my number?

Himan - actually, I give your number to Asim, yesterday me and Asim talking about your relationship. You guys look beautiful together.... So I thought if I give number then your friendship will change into....?

Naaz - what??? How dare you?

Himan - calm down Shehnaz....

Naaz - how can I??? Today he cross his limit....

Himan - why ?

what he did?

Naaz - he even ask me to stay away from Abinandan...

Himan - oh... It's means something...

Naaz - what ???

Himan - how dumb my friend is ? He is posissive about you. I think he is....

Naaz - stop your stupid opinion... Are You trying to brainwash ??

Himan - no no... Not, I am just trying to make you understand...

Naaz - I don't wanna understand anything....

Next day

Himan - hi... Shehnaz

Naaz - hello ? Himan - you're still upset with me ?

Naaz - sss

Himan - oh... I am sorry ?

Naaz - hmm...

Himan - why you didn't receive Sid call?

Naaz - I think it's none of your business... Anyway who told you?

Himan - hmm...Asim.

Naaz - Ssss.... I am coming... Sorry dear, I will see you soon... Abhinandan is calling me ? So... Byeeee

Himan - uff... This girl ?

After some time

Sid - where's she?

Himan - who ??

Sid - hmm... Shehnaz.

Himan - lil bit hesitate to tell but later, "she's with Abhinandan"

Sid - what????

Sid look Asim with tense and they both ask where she went?

Himan - Icc building Sid - fine... Let's go

After few hours

Sid - how dare you to touch my girl?

And he punch his face with full force.

Naaz - hugged him tightly ? And he punch his face with full force.

Naaz - thanks.... I am sorry ?

Sid - didn't I told you to stay away from him....

Naaz - I am sorry ?

Sid - hmm... Ok fine...

. Sid - let me drop you...

Naaz - no thanks... I will go with Himanshi ?

Sid - your wish. Take care ?bye...

Naaz - good bye....

Shehnaz pov

Oh.... My god He told me his girl.... How posissive he is... really ? Should I call him? Or Should I ask sorry ? Oh... He look so handsome when he get angry ? Shut up Shehnaz.

CHAPTER THIRTEEN

What are you thinking? He is my.... No... nothing like that.. He is my friend, no best friend or more than best friend ? How bad Abhinandan is ... I never ever expect from him like this toxic behaviour ? What if Sidharth not come on that moment, what would happen ? Anyway... I don't want to think about past because past is past... I am verry verry thankful to him... I don't know how can I thank him... Oh... This song suits my mood, I think I should put it as status ??

And later she choose a song and uploaded on status.

birthday fun, good bye ?

After some days

Naaz - hi aunty ji...

Mrs Shekhar - hello.... I was waiting for you dear...

Naaz - oh... Why? Mrs Shekhar - I wanna introduce you with someone ☺?

Naaz - oh... I see, who? Mrs Shekhar - guess who ????

Naaz - aunty ji ?..... No idea.

Mrs Shekhar - hmm....fine.

Mrs Shekhar - this is Shehnaz & Shehnaz dear, this is Abhishek ☺?

Naaz - oh... Nice to meet you ?

Abhishek - good to meet you

Mrs Shekhar - ok.... You guys carry on, I am leaving....

Naaz - oh no.... Aunty ji ? You stay here, no problem.

After few minutes

Naaz - aunty ji... Your son wanna talks to you.

Mrs Shekhar - oh good.... Naaz - ok bye...

In college

Naaz - today is my last day in college as well as in Delhi ?

Himan - uff.... I can't live without you dear?

Himan - today Sidharth's birthday, did you wish?

Naaz - how can I forgot ☺? I wished him at sharp 12 'o clock

Himan - really ???

Naaz - why should I tell lie to you? Anyway I am going to his birthday party in evening ?

Himan - hmm...good

In evening

Sid - Asim.... Today I am going to propose her...

Asim - whom???? Oh... Bhabhi

Sid - ? Asim - oh.... You're blushing ? Oh... Bhabhi is coming....

Naaz - hey... Sidharth, once again happy birthday...

Sid - thanks... Anyway you're late for party, everyone left & party is already finished.

Naaz - it's ok... I came here to meet you not everyone or to attend party?

Sid - hmm... Fine ?

Naaz - I wanna tell you something...

Sid - really?? I too

Naaz - what?? Sid - no... Ladies first ?

Naaz - ok... Firstly thanks... For protecting me, secondly today is my last, so .... Good bye.

Sid - ???? Why are you excited????

Naaz - actually, I am gonna meet my family. So I am verry happy...

now tell, you what were going to tell?

Sid - ? nothing.... Just I wanna tell is... Take care....

Naaz - oh... Thanks ? Bye....

Sid - wait... What about help???

Naaz - don't worry Sidharth... I am not one of them who forget their promises ? Wait for some more days

? Sid - ? Good bye... Shehnaz.

Asim - bro.... What about propose?

Sid - I didn't propose her...

Asim - but why???

Sid - I think she don't have any feelings for me, even she didn't look sad...

Asim - so...?

Sid - so... It's not better to not propose her...

Asim - ufff.... you & your logic.

Sid - ? Sid - ok .... Let me sleep it's midnight.

Asim - hmm... Good night

In home

Naaz - I should say goodbye to everyone ....

Mammy (aunt) - I already said you that this bicth * Shehnaz will wins Mrs Shekhar's heart and now she will come as daughter in law ?

Suman - don't worry mom.... She will not.

Naaz - what they are talking about???? Who cares? I don't wanna think about this mystery ?

Naaz - excuse me aunt (aunt) Mammy

(aunt) - ? what???

Naaz - actually, today is my last day in this house, so .... I came here to say goodbye to you both.

Suman - your going ????

Naaz - Ssss Suman - oh... Good to hear ?

Naaz - pardon???

Suman - hmmm... Nothing, good bye.

Mrs Shekhar - today is my son's birthday, I am really missing him?

Mr Shekhar - don't talk about him.... Infront of me.

Mrs Shekhar - don't you miss him???

Mr Shehkar - for me he is dead?

Mrs Shekhar - no... You can't be this heartless.

Mr Shekhar - it's not me it's your son who was heartless, who even not bother to think before murdering my own mother ?

Naaz - in besides the room door ? Oh.... They still stick with this issue ?

Naaz - aunty ji....

Mrs Shekhar - Ssss my dear, come in.

Naaz - actually, today is my last day in this house ? So... good bye to everyone

Mrs Shekhar - why are you talking like this??? I'll miss you so much dear. And she started crying.

You can come home when ever you want ?

Mir Shekhar - take care dear? Good bye...

Naaz - hmm... she also get emotional Bye...

Naaz - Naina.... Where's Naina?

Servant - actually, she's in her leave.

Naaz - ufff.... Ok I will call her later.

Bye... Everyone ??

CHAPTER FOURTEEN

Abhishek or Sidharth ?

After few months

Mrs Shekhar - I think we should go Shehnaz house today and ask her hand for our son... Abhishek

Mr Shekhar - yeah... It's a good idea but you should ask Abhishek first he's coming India Today.

Mrs Shekhar - no need... Because I think he also like her, so... We should give surprise.

Mr Shekhar - hmm...? Ok... I am telling to my friend (Shehnaz's father).

I think he will agree...

After some time

Shehnaz father - hello Shehnaz be ready some special guest are coming.?

In Bombay

Naaz - hello... Sidharth

Sid - hi... Shehnaz, today I am coming Bombay to meet you.

Naaz - oh really........

Sid - ☺?

Naaz - ok... I am lil bit busy, some special guest are coming....

Sid - who???

Naaz - I don't know, dad said special guest that's all ?

Sid - hmm.... Sid - hello... Shehnaz I am on the way to your home ?

Sid - ufff... what I am I seeing???

My family and even Abhishek.... Is coming to Shehnaz house. Why they're coming??? Oh... They're the special guest ?

Sid - hello Asim (...........)

Asim - what??? Your family is in Shehnaz house. It's means.... They were going to ask Shehnaz hand ?

This Shehnaz gold digger ? She cheats you.... She take every favour from you.... When it comes to marriage she choses Abhishek instead of you.... Hello... Hello... Are you there ??? Sidharth...

Asim - uff... He already cuts the call...

Himan - how dare you to tell my friend gold digger???

Asim - oh... I am Just saving my friend.

Himan - you were not saving him, you're just separating them ?

Himan - even your friend is rude, arrogant, heartless ....etc

Asim - hey.... What are you saying??

Himan - I am saying the truth, remember truth always seems bitter ?

Asim - leave it... I don't wanna talk to you.

Himan - oh... Hello I am also not dying to talk ? Byeee...
In house

Naaz - namaste ? uncle aunty ji

Mr & Mrs Shekhar - Good bless you ☺? Dear

. Mrs Shekhar - don't you know, why we are here ?

Naaz - hmm.... No.

Mrs Shekhar - actually, we are here to ask your hand for Abhishek.

Naaz - she's shock as hell, her voice get stuck in her throat.

she can't believe in her own ears.

Abhishek - what?????

he also get shock, what you mean???

finally ?

Abhishek - Sorry mom.... I can't, I love another girl in Australia.... Now she's coming and I was about to meet her,to you all

Mrs Shekhar - what???

That day you said she's awesome... Now what happen??

Abhishek - I told the truth, that she's awesome. It never ever mean I like her.

Everyone - got shock

Naaz - I would like to give you all, another shock....

She went out and bring Sidharth from outside....

Naaz - now... Look at here carefully ?

Aunt - why you brought this devil?

Naaz - everyone get to know, who's actual devil

This is a pendrive let me connect this to my laptop. To show you all a happy movie ? May be for someone it's horror... But just adjust it... (*The dark secret revealed* ....)

Mr & Mrs Shekhar - I am sorry my son... we didn't believe you . . .

Mrs Shekhar - Sidharth ...

do you know, how much I miss you???

I am really sorry, we're feeling very guilty.

Mr Shekhar - I am really sorry my friend for Abhishek's sudden behaviour

We can't... engage with your daugter.

Mrs Shekhar - no... We can ask Shehnaz hand for my son ..... Sidharth Shukla

If you don't have any problem my brother (Shehnaz father)

Shehnaz father - no... No.. but first ask your son

Mrs Shekhar - I know my son always respect my words... So... My son are you agree with my decision ?

Sid - he feels like he is in ninth cloud.

I am okay But .... Ask Shehnaz...

Naaz - I am agree with my father's decission

Oh.... Finally engaged.

TO BE CONTINUED . . .

Meet you in next part.